Cayuga Island Kids

The Case of the Messy Message and the Missing Facts

Story by
Judy Bradbury

Illustrations by
Gabriella Vagnoli

A City of Light imprint

© 2022 Text by Judy Bradbury
© 2022 Illustrations by Gabriella Vagnoli

All rights reserved. No part of this publication may be reproduced, distributed, or transmitted in any form or by any means, including photocopying, recording, or other electronic or mechanical means, without the prior permission of the publisher, except in the case of brief quotations embodied in reviews and other noncommercial uses permitted by copyright law. For permission requests, contact the publisher.

 Cross Your Fingers
A City of Light imprint

 City of Light Publishing
266 Elmwood Ave. Suite 407
Buffalo, New York 14222

info@CityofLightPublishing.com
www.CityofLightPublishing.com

Written by Judy Bradbury
Illustrated by Gabriella Vagnoli
Book design by Ana Cristina Ochoa

ISBN 978-1-952536-31-1 (softcover)
ISBN 978-1-952536-32-8 (hardcover)
ISBN 978-1-952536-33-5 (eBook)

10 9 8 7 6 5 4 3 2 1

Library of Congress Cataloging-in-Publication Data

Names: Bradbury, Judy, author. | Vagnoli, Gabriella, 1979- illustrator.
Title: The case of the messy message and the missing facts / story by Judy Bradbury ; illustrations by Gabriella Vagnoli.
Description: Buffalo, New York : Cross Your Fingers, a City of Light imprint, [2022] | Series: Cayuga Island kids ; Book 3 | Audience: Ages 7-10. | Audience: Grades 2-3. | Summary: The Cayuga Island Kids learn about sorting through research and clues to ensure information is factual as they deal with faulty assumptions, missing facts, flour bugs, and chocolate chip cookies.
Identifiers: LCCN 2021056075 (print) | LCCN 2021056076 (ebook) | ISBN 9781952536328 (hardcover) | ISBN 9781952536311 (trade paperback) | ISBN 9781952536335 (ebook) | ISBN 9781952536335 (epub) | ISBN 9781952536335 (kindle edition) | ISBN 9781952536335 (mobi) | ISBN 9781952536335 (pdf)
Subjects: CYAC: Mystery and detective stories. | Research--Fiction. | Facts (Philosophy)--Fiction. | Truth--Fiction. | LCGFT: Novels.
Classification: LCC PZ7.B71645 Cas 2022 (print) | LCC PZ7.B71645 (ebook) | DDC [Fic]--dc23
LC record available at https://lccn.loc.gov/2021056075
LC ebook record available at https://lccn.loc.gov/2021056076

To the Cayuga Island Kids, past, present, and future.

~ Judy

The Cayuga Island Kids

LACEY

MAC

Other Cayuga Island Characters

MR. ESPOSITO

MRS. SCHIEBER

MS. CHOI

JULIAN MAYA YOKO

MADDIE TAISHI

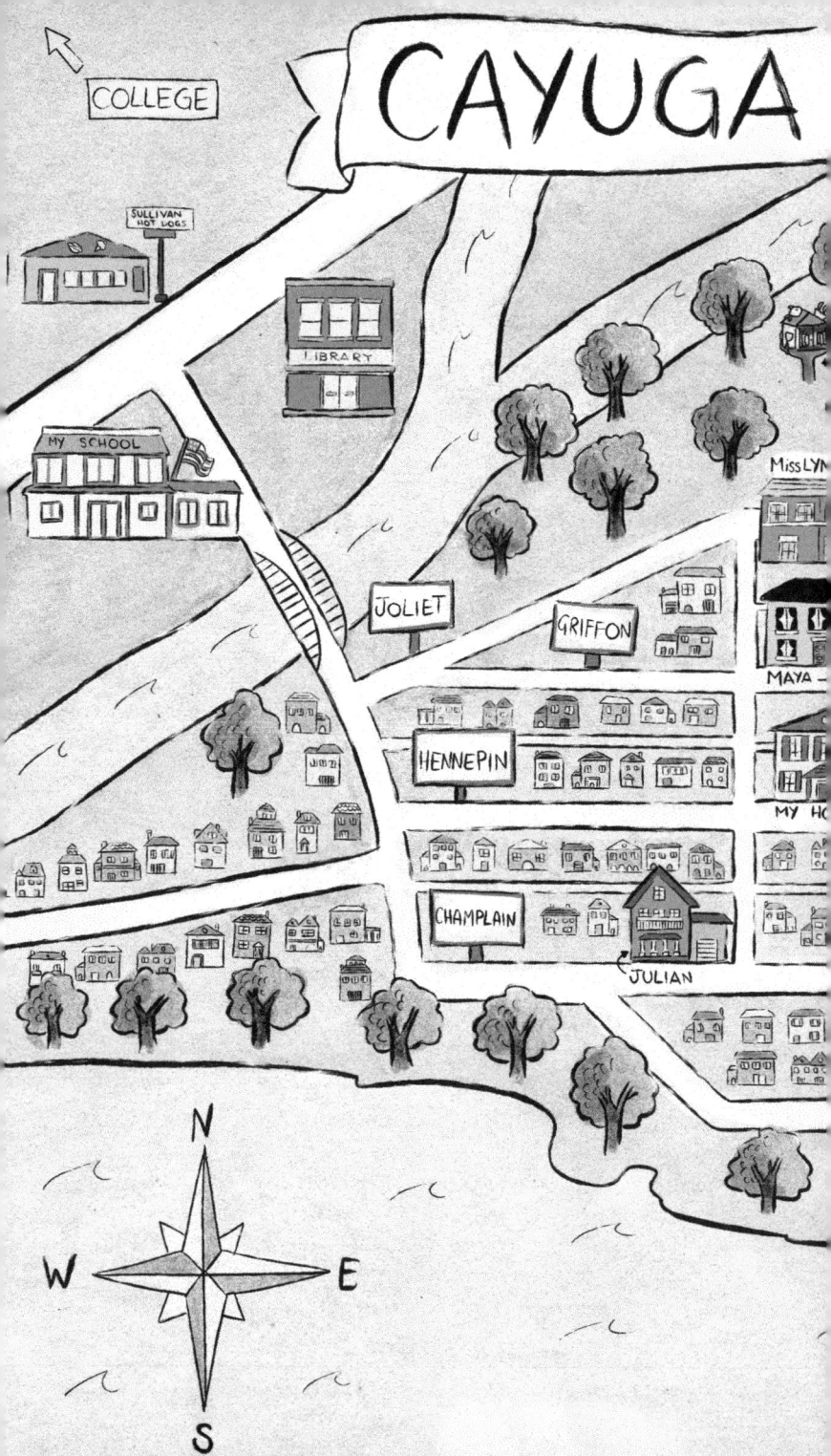

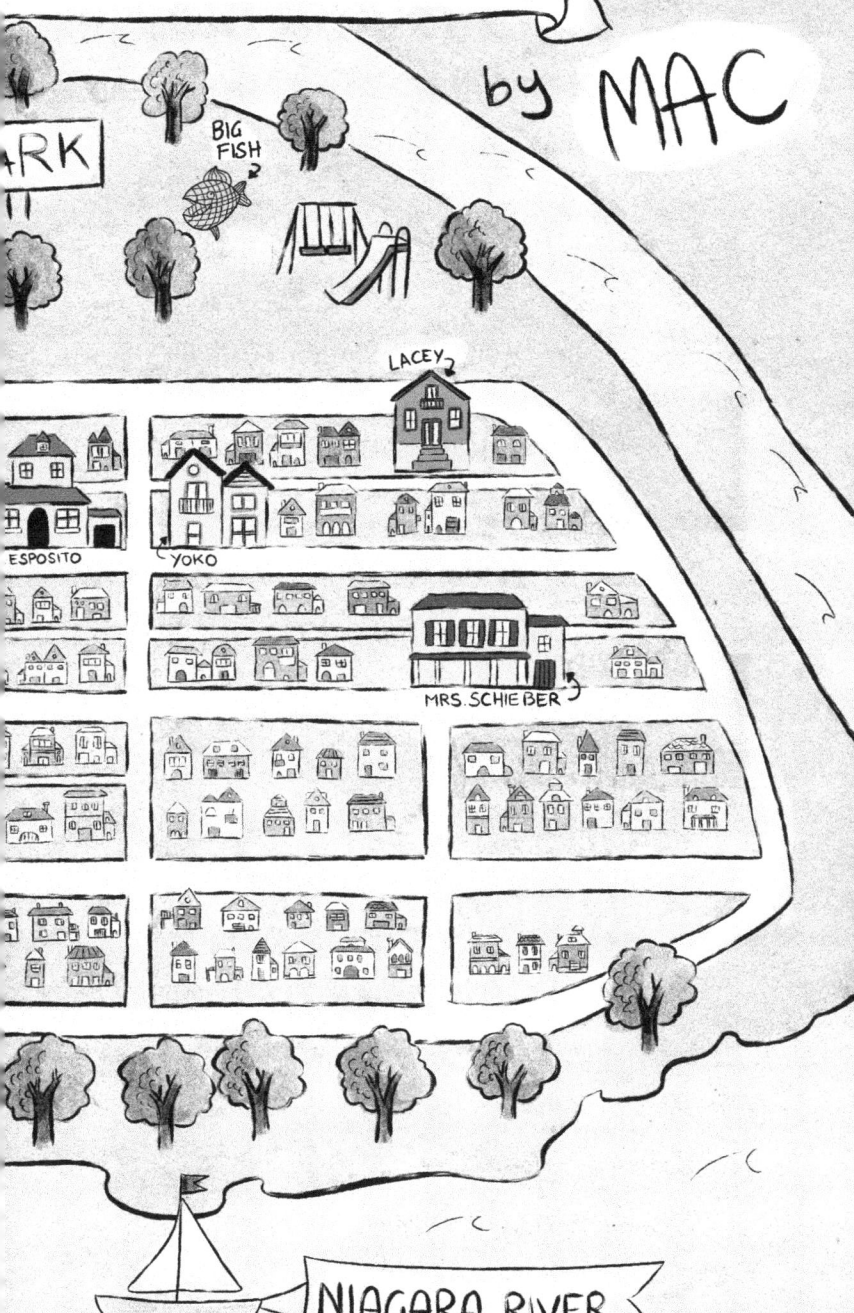

Cayuga Island Kids

Cayuga Island is just a few miles upstream from the mighty Niagara Falls, one of the Seven Wonders of the World. A narrow bridge leads on and off this tiny island. It crosses where the churning Niagara River narrows to a gurgling creek.

Four streets run the length of the island. Three are named for explorers of the Niagara Frontier. The fourth street is named after the Griffon, a ship with a mysterious history. Gravel alleys wind behind the houses.

But there are no schools or stores, no stoplights or movie theaters, or much of anything else on the island—except fun, adventure, and perhaps a bit of mystery, if you look for it.

It's fall now, and that means school and homework for the Cayuga Island Kids—Lacey, Mac, Julian, Maya, and Yoko. But there's still plenty of time for adventure, and even a bit of mystery.

Are you ready? Come along and join the fun!

Contents

1	The Cayuga Island Kids	1
2	Practice	12
3	Missing	19
4	Cookie Research	28
5	Specks	32
6	Flour Facts	36
7	Messy Message	42
8	Research Explorers	47
9	Clues	55
10	Plans	61
11	Mis- Dis- Information	65
12	Fact Detectives	69
13	Suspect	74
14	Meet at the Scene	80
15	Feeling Good	85
16	Clue Review	90
17	Important?	96
18	Fraction of the Truth	101
19	Mystery Solved	107
20	Kindness Rocks	113

My childhood is a part of my story,

and it's why I'm who I am today

and why my career is what it is.

~ Misty Copeland

Chapter One
The Cayuga Island Kids

For Lacey, one of the best parts of a new school year happens a few weeks before classes begin.

Store shelves overflow with school supplies.

Backpacks.

Scented markers.

Neon flexible rulers.

Pens with funny caps, like a kangaroo on a spring.

And best of all, shelves brim with notebooks in every possible size, shape, and design.

Lacey loves school supplies.

Gram knew this. That's why at the store, she reminded Lacey, "Let's keep to the essentials." Lacey held the list provided by the teachers. Gram pointed to the shopping cart. "Only items you absolutely need end up here."

Lacey walked up and down the school supplies aisles. She investigated, as all good detectives do. On a bottom shelf, she discovered bundled packs of notebooks. Lacey counted. There were enough for each subject, plus one extra. She did the math. The bundle was cheaper than buying single notebooks.

Lacey suggested they place the extra notebook in the Little Free Library that Gram had built for Cayuga Island Park. "I'll label it, 'Little Free Library Sharing Notebook.' Visitors can write messages about the books they like."

Gram approved, and they checked *notebooks* off the list.

Next, Lacey hefted a twelve pack of tissues into the cart. Each student had to bring in nine boxes. Lacey suggested they donate the extras to the pantry at the community center.

Gram had a coupon for a bonus pack of colored pencils.

Lacey found a reusable lunch bag with a mail-in rebate.

With all they saved, Lacey was able to convince Gram to let her add a nifty pen with three colors of ink to the cart. Three pens in one! "It's not essential," Lacey admitted, "but it's perfect for organizing."

Lacey didn't mention what she intended to organize, but Gram agreed, and the pen made it into the cart. At the register, Gram plucked a small spiral notebook from a wire bin and added it to their pile of school supplies. "That's for your pocket," she said with a wink.

Lacey was ready for school. She was also ready for a fall full of mystery and adventure. She had a pen with three colors of ink. She could use a different color for clues, questions, and notes in her new pocket notebook.

For Mac, one of the best parts of starting the school year was his new Wild Frontier lunch box. Well, it was new to him, even though it was almost as old as Uncle Anthony. It was his when he was Mac's age.

The lunch box was made of metal with a curved plastic handle. It even had a thermos tucked inside. There was only one small dent on the bottom corner. Uncle Anthony's eyes twinkled when he said, "That gives it character."

Mac agreed.

Mac's dad showed him how to rub away patches of rust along the edges of the lunch box. They scrubbed the handle and the thermos with baking soda.

Mac was glad that his new lunch box still looked old, just like his powder horn and coonskin cap. Those were his dad's when he was a kid, and now they were Mac's. He couldn't wear his cap to school, and he couldn't take along his powder horn, but every time he opened his desk, he could peek at his Wild Frontier lunch box. No matter what vegetable slices his mom made sure he packed inside, his new old lunch box reminded him that adventures awaited.

Julian liked pretty much everything about a new school year. His friends met up at the bus stop. The school playground not only had climbing equipment, it had bird feeders, a sun dial, a vegetable patch, and even a bee and butterfly garden.

A new school year meant learning new things. Julian was curious, and he liked facts. Science was always his favorite subject, but after discovering the history of Cayuga Island last summer, Julian was eager for Social Studies, too. And this year, he had library class twice a week.

Mrs. Schieber was the school librarian, and she made research come alive. She was also a Cayuga Island neighbor. Last summer she helped the Cayuga Island Kids solve a mystery. She also baked the yummiest chocolate chip cookies ever for the Big Fish community project.

Since then, Julian and his dad had been trying to match her chocolate chip cookie goodness. Sure, they could have asked Mrs. Schieber for her recipe, but they decided it was more fun to experiment. Julian's friends liked being the samplers. Julian kept notes on all the recipes and his friends' comments on his tablet.

"We won't give up," Julian's dad declared. "Our recipe might be off by just a pinch of this or a tad of that!"

One of the words on Julian's *Junior Scientist's Word-of-the-Day* calendar was hypothesis. It means, "an explanation used in further investigation." Julian liked his dad's cookie recipe hypothesis. Further investigations were tasty!

Maya looked forward to the after-school activities. This year she was a helper in Ms. Choi's weekly craft club for younger students. The Make-and-Take Club met in the art room, which was Maya's most favorite classroom.

Maya's other most favorite classroom was the auditorium. It wasn't really a classroom, but it was where dance class happened. Right on the stage! It was perfect, because it was wood and it was wide. And since they danced on the stage all year, it wasn't scary being up there when it was time for the recital!

This year, Maya's dance class met twice a week. That meant she could wear all of her most favorite leotards more often. And maybe, just maybe, she'd be ready for en pointe work soon. Maya couldn't wait to get up on the tips of her toes!

Maya also met up with her friends after school in Cayuga Island Park. Last summer they made a big discovery right in the middle of a flower bed! They also planned a community project.

Maya's mom said, "You and your friends hit it out of the park." She was being funny, because the project took place in the park. But Maya knew her mom was proud of what they accomplished.

Now that it was fall, the Cayuga Island Kids couldn't meet in the park as often, but Maya was certain there was still plenty of time for adventure.

"A new school year is like a pile of wrapped packages," Yoko told her friends the week before school started. "It's full of surprises."

Yoko liked making comparisons. She thought that one up when the school supply list arrived. In the upper left-hand corner beside her grade and room number, she discovered a big surprise.

"I'm in Mr. Robinson's class!" Yoko announced.

"Lucky," Mac said. He and Julian had Ms. Spritski. She was the strictest teacher in their school. No running in the hallways. No outside voices when she was around.

Yoko agreed with Mac.

Mr. Robinson led a lunchroom poetry slam. Yoko loved poetry. Even her name rhymed!

Mr. Robinson dressed like characters in books, and not only on Halloween.

Yoko loved to read. After all, she was going to be an author someday.

And Mr. Robinson was in charge of the school play.

Yoko planned to practice learning lines for the play. She would memorize homework pages and cafeteria menus. Then, when it was time to learn her part in the play, it would be as easy as tying sneakers.

Yoko knew from summer camp that acting is more than saying lines. Gestures and facial expressions— how we move our hands and arms, and the look on our faces—give clues to what we are feeling or thinking, even if we don't say a word. Yoko planned to practice those, too.

Yoko's mind bubbled with plans for a school year full of adventure.

CHAPTER TWO

Practice

After school, Julian stepped in line for the bus with the big **CI**—for Cayuga Island—in the window. The sun glinted off the wide windshield. He noticed leaves on a few trees were beginning to change color.

Do all leaves change color in the fall? Julian wondered. *Why are some leaves more colorful than others? Are the first trees to bud in the spring the first to lose their leaves in the fall? Or the last?*

Julian's thoughts shifted when he spotted Yoko. Her mouth was turned down. Her eyebrows bunched. Her hands made tight fists as she stamped toward the bus.

Practice

Julian left the line and hurried to meet her. "What's wrong?" he asked. "You look angry."

Suddenly, Yoko's frown disappeared and her eyes brightened. She pumped the air. "Yes!" she exclaimed.

Now it was Julian's eyebrows that bunched. Only he wasn't upset. He was puzzled.

"I'm practicing," Yoko announced.

"You're practicing being mad?"

"I'm practicing *looking* mad," Yoko explained as she stepped in line. "I think I nailed it."

"Are you practicing *looking* glad now?" Julian asked. "Or are you really glad?"

That's when Mac caught up to them. "Really glad about what?" he asked.

"I'm glad Julian thought I was upset even though I wasn't," Yoko answered.

"Wait. What?" Mac rubbed his head. He was almost as confused as he had been when his teacher was explaining fractions. Even though Ms. Spritski used a plastic pizza, fractions were not appealing. They muddled his brain.

"I'm practicing gestures and facial expressions," Yoko continued as they moved up in the bus line. "I'm going to try out for the school play."

Mac didn't know exactly what gestures were. But he figured facial expressions were what you did with your face—smiles and frowns, a grin, and maybe sticking out your tongue. "Julian thought you were mad, but you were glad. Did you mix up your faces?"

The friends giggled as they climbed the bus steps. Mac paused when he reached the driver. He dug into his backpack and offered Mrs. O'Doodle the snack pack of carrots from his lunch.

She jiggled the package. "Carrots are crammed with goodness, you know."

Mac ducked his head. "I was full."

Mrs. O'Doodle eyed Mac as she placed the carrots in the netted pocket on the side of the driver's seat. "It's kind of you to think of me." Then she leaned toward Mac and patted his shoulder. "Carrots get better the more you eat them."

Mac claimed the seat in front of Yoko and Julian. When Lacey boarded the bus, he waved and pointed to the seat beside him.

"No homework!" Lacey pumped her fist in the air. She slid into the seat beside Mac and turned to face her friends. "Maya has Make-and-Take Club, but she can meet us in the park afterwards." Maya was in Lacey's class, so that meant she didn't have homework, either. "I just have to put the cut-up vegetables in the pot for our soup tonight. Then I can head over."

"I could have saved you some time," Mac said. "I had carrots in my lunch."

"Mmm. Carrots are so crunchy." Lacey smacked her lips.

Mac shrugged. "I was full. I gave them to Mrs. O'Doodle."

Suddenly, Yoko moaned. She held her mouth. She placed her forehead on the back of Lacey's seat.

Mac peered at her. "You don't like carrots, either?"

Yoko took a deep breath and exhaled. "Oooh." She rubbed her stomach.

Lacey put her hand on Yoko's shoulder. "Do you feel sick?"

Yoko's head popped up. "I'm fine!" She swung her legs and bounced in her seat.

"She was *practicing*." Julian eyed Yoko. "Right?"

Lacey looked from Julian to Yoko. "You were practicing feeling sick?"

"Voices down! Back pockets, meet the seats! Buckle up, buckaroos. This bronco is leaving the chute!" Mrs. O'Doodle bellowed from the front of the bus.

Yoko sat back. "I'll tell you all about it at the park," she promised Lacey.

"We have homework." Mac pointed to himself and Julian. "Fractions." He groaned, and he wasn't practicing. He really was feeling bad about that.

"We can work on our homework together," Julian offered. "We'll use chocolate chip cookies to figure out the problems."

Mac brightened. "I am a little hungry."

"Mac, my friend! Feet on the floor. Face

forward!" Mrs. O'Doodle didn't have eyes in the back of her head. But she did have a big mirror aimed at the rows of students behind her.

Mac settled beside Lacey. The door squeaked closed and the bus rumbled away from the curb.

Chapter Three
Missing

At the park, Pesky was being pesky, so Lacey placed a treat for him on the ground. She held her hand up. "Wait," she commanded.

While Pesky focused on the biscuit, Lacey turned her attention back to Maya.

"...So while Ms. Choi explained to the little kids how to make a greeting card, I passed out the supplies. I collected them at the end of the meeting. Ms. Choi and I were putting everything away when we noticed two glitter pens were missing."

"Missing?" Lacey leaned forward. This sounded mysterious. "Did you check under the tables?" she asked. "How about the trash can? Could someone have thrown them out because they were used up?"

Maya picked up a maple leaf that had fallen to the ground. "We checked the floor, the trash can, and even the chairs." She followed the outline of the maple leaf with her finger. "We didn't find them."

Lacey patted Pesky's head and pointed to the treat. "Okay!" His tail wagged as he pounced on the biscuit. She pulled her notebook from her pocket. At the top of the page in red ink, she wrote

Make-and-Take Club Mystery

She clicked to the blue ink. "Begin at the beginning. Tell me everything." She paused. "Give me the *important* details."

"I just did," said Maya.

Lacey's pen hung over the notebook. "How do you know that two glitter pens were missing?"

Maya looked up at the maple tree, thinking. "Ms. Choi had a check-in list. Before the kids came in, we counted out two glitter pens, one piece of cardstock, and a glue stick for each person."

Maya snapped her fingers. "We also filled bowls with decorations. Two bowls for each table. The pieces were all different shapes and colors!" Maya paused. "But I guess that isn't important."

"Probably not," Lacey said. She waited for her friend to continue.

"While Ms. Choi showed examples of greeting card designs, I passed out the supplies. Except the paper towels." Maya tapped Lacey's notebook. "I forgot to tell you about those. They were for cleanup at the end of the meeting." Maya took a breath. "Anyway, after Ms. Choi answered questions, everyone got busy."

Lacey flipped to a new page in her notebook. "What happened after they made their cards?"

"We had Show and Tell. Then we put the cards in baggies so they'd be safe in their backpacks." Maya stood and stretched. She circled her head with her arms and twirled. When she noticed Lacey was waiting, she continued. "Everyone passed the glitter pens and glue sticks to me. Ms. Choi collected the bowls. I helped wipe down the tables. Little kids aren't that good at clean up." Maya's head bobbed. "They hung up their aprons and then they left." Maya stopped. "I forgot to tell you. Ms. Choi has aprons for the kids to wear so their clothes don't get dirty. Little kids aren't that good at crafts." Maya bent her knees and straightened. Then she twirled again. "I'm pretty sure that's everything."

"How did you figure out what was missing?" Lacey asked.

"After the kids left, Ms. Choi and I put away the supplies. That's when we realized glitter pens were missing. There were two empty spaces in the trays." Maya sighed. "We looked everywhere. Ms. Choi even checked her apron pockets!"

Lacey clicked from blue ink to green ink. In her notebook she wrote

** What happened to the missing glitter pens??? **

Lacey promised Maya she would think about the Make-and-Take Club Mystery.

By the time Julian and Mac arrived at the park, Yoko was playing fetch with Pesky.

Mac looked around. The big rocks along the creek were waiting to be hopped across. He spotted their neighbor. Mr. Esposito volunteered as the Cayuga Island Park groundskeeper. He mowed, he weeded, he planted flowers. Today he was raking around the Little Free Library. Down the path, the late afternoon sun slanted across the peak on the playground castle.

"Adventures await!" Mac announced to his friends.

"And a mystery." Lacey patted the pocket holding her notebook.

"We'll explain later," Maya said as she hopped up. "Ready! Set! Go!"

The friends raced to the playground.

Pesky won.

Chapter Four
Cookie Research

After dinner, Julian and his dad tried a new chocolate chip cookie recipe. While the cookies baked, Julian made notes about the recipe on his tablet. Then they worked as a team to clean up the kitchen.

Julian's father placed the scoop in the flour bin and popped on the lid. It made a snapping sound. It was good to go. He slid the canister down the counter.

Julian stood ready with a damp towel. He caught the canister and spun it as he wiped away flour dust. When he was finished, he slid it back to his dad. The sugar tin was next.

Cookie Research

Meanwhile, the timer ticked. When it dinged, Julian and his dad stood side by side at the oven. They eased open the door and peeked inside.

Were the edges golden? Was it time to slide the baking sheet out of the oven?

Julian's glasses fogged from the heat. "Your call, Dad!" He removed his glasses and waved them in the air.

Once the cookies had cooled, Julian's dad lifted two from the rack.

They inspected the cookies. "The color is great," Julian said, reaching for his tablet. "They're not too dark, but not too light, either."

They each took a bite.

"The chips are gooey. I like that," Julian noted.

"It's hard to complain about a warm cookie." Julian's dad smacked his lips. "But—for research purposes—the edges are flat and crunchy while the middle is a little too chewy."

Julian knew from reading on the internet that there are variables when baking cookies. Food science. Ingredients and methods make a difference. He clicked to the cookie chart he had saved on his tablet. Flat, crunchy edges and a chewy middle might mean they needed to adjust the amount of baking powder and baking soda.

Julian's dad brushed crumbs from the corner of his mouth. He looked up and pointed to a wet spot on the ceiling. "Cookie research is way better than water leak research. I'm off to the attic to investigate."

"I'll finish cleaning up," Julian offered.

When his dad removed his apron, he found a measuring spoon in the pocket. He tossed it to Julian and headed up the stairs.

Julian washed the bowl and spoons and wiped down the counters. He chose a plump cookie to tuck in his dad's lunch sack. Next, he wrapped five cookies—one to share with each of his friends tomorrow, and one for himself. Then he wrapped one more. You never knew who might need a cookie.

Chapter Five
Specks

At the lunch table the next day, Yoko gladly accepted Mac's carrots. She placed each round slice between two of her cucumber slices to make tiny sandwiches. She offered one to Mac, but he shook his head. Julian was passing out cookies.

"Samplers, you have work to do," Julian joked. "Let me know what you think of this batch."

Julian was powering up his tablet to take notes when Maddie Pratt came by their table. She was on her way to return her lunch tray. A half-eaten snack pie lay crumbled in the corner. When Maddie spotted the chocolate chip cookies, she stopped. "Did you buy those here?" she asked. She forgot to say hi first.

"Julian and his dad baked them," Maya answered. "Don't they look delicious?"

Julian reached in his lunch bag for the extra cookie. He slid his chair over to make room. Maddie could be a sampler, too.

But Maddie didn't seem to notice. And she forgot to answer Maya.

She leaned over Lacey's shoulder. Her tray tilted. The plastic fork skated toward the edge. Her bangs fell forward as she took a closer look.

"There are specks in those cookies." Maddie's milk carton tipped and dribbled over the corner of the tray. "I bet they're bugs! Flour bugs!" Her voice rose. "They look just like a picture I saw on the internet!"

Lacey put her hand up to steady the tray. "What are you talking about, Maddie?" She brushed a few drops of milk from her sleeve.

Maddie stepped back. She looked from the cookies to Julian. One side of her mouth lifted and her eyebrow arched. She pointed to Julian's tablet. "Look it up. You'll see!"

Mac put down his cookie.

Maya held her napkin up and wiped a bit of cookie from her mouth.

Julian's cheeks burned. Maddie wasn't the friendliest kid in school. She could be bossy, and she liked things her way. But she wasn't mean. He didn't think she would say something just to hurt someone's feelings.

Meanwhile, Yoko watched their classmate walk away. Maddie's shoulders hunched and she shuddered. After she cleared her tray, she whispered to Minh, who was waiting in line behind her. Minh's eyes widened. Her mouth formed an O. She looked toward Julian and wrinkled her nose.

Chapter Six
Flour Facts

After school, Lacey gathered books to donate to the Little Free Library. She weeded three mysteries she had finished from her bookshelf headboard. She dusted off two more she found under her bed. Gram added a thick biography and a few magazines to the stack.

Lacey piled everything into a cloth grocery bag and hefted it over her shoulder. "Maya and I will stop at the park on our way home from Julian's house," she told Gram.

Once they had all arrived, the kids gathered at the island in Julian's kitchen. In front of them were the remaining cookies from the batch and the flour canister.

Julian had loaded three websites on his tablet. Each offered information about flour bugs. Julian knew that just because something was on the internet didn't make it true. That's why he always checked more than one source.

"Flour bugs are common," he reported. "And they won't hurt you if they're baked into your food."

"That's good news." Mac eyed the cookies. "I guess."

Julian continued reading. "There are ways to avoid flour bugs. Putting flour in the freezer for a few days after you buy it works. So does storing flour in an airtight container."

Yoko reached for the flour canister and popped off the top. "This lid is as tight as a new pair of dress shoes." She peered inside the bin. "What do flour bugs look like?"

Julian clicked to images of flour bugs.

"Ewwww!" Maya's forehead rumpled.

Lacey read the caption. "These pictures are magnified. Flour bugs are tiny, but you can see them. They look like brown specks."

"And the specks in the flour will be moving," Julian added.

Specks. Mac recalled that was the word Maddie had used when she saw the cookies. His mouth soured. Learning about flour bugs was definitely ruining his appetite for cookies.

But when his friends leaned over the canister, he did, too. Searching for flour bugs was sort of an adventure.

Julian dug into the flour with the scoop. He pushed it around. No specks. "I have an idea." Julian opened a drawer and took out a roll of waxed paper. "Let's spread some flour out and see if we discover any bugs."

Lacey pulled out her magnifying glass. Maya flipped on another set of kitchen lights. The kids examined the fluffy mound. It was dusty, but it was pure white.

"No bugs," declared Yoko. She brushed one hand against the other as if to say, "That's that!"

The side door squeaked and Julian's dad walked into the kitchen. He placed his lunch sack by the sink and gave Julian a shoulder hug. "Thanks for the surprise cookie. Lots of chunks of chocolate." He gestured a thumbs up, and then he noticed the flour on the counter. "Are you making another batch already?"

Julian told his dad about Maddie and the cookie specks. He showed him the flour bug images. His father held up his hand and shook his head.

"This bin is old and dented, but it's sturdy and airtight." He patted the canister and smiled at the kids. "It belonged to Julian's grandfather, my father. He wasn't much for cookies, but I learned to bake bread from him when I was about your age." He paused. "On Saturday mornings, we bought flour from a mill. When we brought it home, we placed it in the freezer. Our flour comes from the grocery store," he continued, "but I still freeze it for a few days." He looked from Julian to his friends. "Chances are slim we have flour bugs."

"Phew!" Mac reached for one of the cookies. He wouldn't be giving them up after all.

"What could have caused the specks?" Lacey asked.

Julian's face lit up. "I should have thought of

this before!" He clicked to a saved image on his tablet. "I'll check the cookie variable chart."

It didn't take long to find an answer. There was even a photograph. "Small brown spots can occur from over baking," he read. "Lower the temperature by 25 degrees."

Yoko sat back. She was glad for Julian, but she was troubled, too.

"Maddie jumped to conclusions about Julian's cookies. The wrong conclusions," Yoko said. "Then she told Minh. And from the look on Minh's face, I'm pretty sure she believed Maddie."

Lacey shook her head and sputtered.

Yoko hesitated, looking at her friends. "After Maddie left our table, none of us ate the cookies."

Julian nodded. It was true.

Yoko spoke softly. "We all believed Maddie. We jumped to conclusions, too."

Chapter Seven
Messy Message

At the park, Lacey and Maya waved to Mr. Esposito. Today, he was clearing branches from along the creek. A jumbo bag of plastic bottles was stuffed into the back of his golf cart-turned-gardening cart. When they passed by the big fish recycling bin, it was no mystery that it was empty.

Lacey unlatched the door of the Little Free Library and straightened the few items remaining on the shelves. Anyone was welcome to take a book or leave a book. The book-sharing box was popular.

Lacey unpacked the bag and placed the books and magazines she had brought from

Messy Message

home inside the box. Maya held out a beginner's craft book and two fairy tales. Lacey placed them on the shelf. Finally, she pulled out the sharing notebook. Reading what people wrote about the books they borrowed was one of Lacey's favorite parts of taking care of the Little Free Library.

She noticed that the pen she had clipped to the notebook was missing. Again. Lacey dug in her bag. "I'm running out of pens," she said. "They always seem to get lost or broken."

"I'll think of a way to attach the pen to the notebook," Maya offered. "I can brainstorm ideas with Ms. Choi."

Lacey knew she could count on Maya to come up with the perfect solution.

The girls leaned over the notebook as Lacey flipped through the pages. She paused when she landed on a message she hadn't read before.

"Vincent liked a book about sunfish." Lacey laughed. "He's hoping it's okay if he keeps it until he has to write a book report."

Lacey flipped the page and found two sheets stuck together. Carefully, she peeled them apart.

Maya squinted at the blurred words. "This message is written with a glitter pen. Whoever wrote it didn't let the ink dry before closing the notebook."

Lacey pulled out her magnifying glass to see if that would help. But all the girls could make out was

Messy Message

"I bet this person read one of the Pet Care Adventure books Yoko donated," Maya guessed.

"I wish we could read the whole note. But at least this person had something to write with." Lacey tucked the sharing notebook into the library and closed the door.

"Wait a minute!" Quickly, Lacey flipped up the latch and reached back inside the library. She pulled out the notebook and opened to the crinkled page. "This message is written in *glitter pen*."

Maya gasped. She was pretty sure they were both thinking the same thought.

Was the note written with one of Ms. Choi's missing glitter pens?

CHAPTER EIGHT

Research Explorers

Mrs. Schieber stood at the door to the library. She welcomed each student with a special greeting. She bowed, fist-bumped, saluted, and hive-fived. She curtsied with Maya and tapped her pen against Lacey's. Students smiled as they took their seats at the long library tables.

Mrs. Schieber had loaded a website on the board. Across the top in curvy letters it said

All About Explorers

Below that was an image of a compass.

Julian sat close to the front. Mrs. Schieber was not only kind and funny, she also liked facts, just like Julian. Mrs. Schieber knew something about everything. She was the school librarian, after all.

The room quieted as Mrs. Schieber stepped to the board. "Let's begin by reviewing what we know about research and fact-finding."

Julian raised his hand. "Always check more than one source," he said. "See if the information is the same."

"Check more than just the internet." Cami pointed toward the library shelves. "Look in books, too."

Maya raised her hand. "Just because you read something online doesn't make it true."

"Same with books!" Jeffrey Joe called out.

"Don't believe everything you hear, either." Yoko looked across the room to Minh. "Just because someone says something doesn't make it true."

Lacey held her pen up. "Be a fact detective!"

"I like that! It sums up what everyone has said." Mrs. Schieber tipped her pen toward Lacey.

"Today, we begin our research projects." Mrs. Schieber moved to the board. "By now you know of my interest in explorers. After all, I live on Cayuga Island. My street is named after Father Louis Hennepin."

She began walking among the tables. "Hundreds of years ago, Hennepin was the first person to see and describe Niagara Falls. The clothespin used to be called a hen's pin. It was named after Hennepin because he invented a way to dry clothes on board the ship during explorations. He even wrote a book called *A New Discovery*."

Mrs. Schieber paused. "Do you agree that researching explorers will be exciting?" she asked.

Students signaled with a thumbs-up. Feet tucked under chairs began swinging.

Mrs. Schieber looked across the room. "What did you find interesting about Father Hennepin?"

Hands waved. When Mrs. Schieber called on students, they recited something she had told them.

Next Mrs. Schieber asked, "How do you know that what I told you about Father Hennepin is true?"

"Because you're our teacher!" exclaimed Maddie.

"Because you live on Hennepin Avenue?" Chara offered.

"I live there, too!" Mac added, even though that didn't answer Mrs. Schieber's question.

"We know you're interested in explorers," said Jeffrey Joe. "And you read a lot!"

"I am your teacher. I live on Hennepin Avenue. Indeed, I am interested in explorers." Mrs. Schieber's eyes glittered. "And I do love to read."

She looked from table to table. "But none of those facts guarantee that what I told you about Father Hennepin is factual."

Mrs. Schieber clicked a button and a list of reminders appeared on the board.

LOOK CLOSELY AT INFORMATION YOU FIND.

INVESTIGATE MORE THAN ONE SOURCE.

CHECK THE FACTS.

Mrs. Schieber summed up. "Be wise research explorers as you research your explorers." She paused so the class could enjoy the way she played with the words.

Mac raised his hand. "Was there something you told us about Father Hennepin that wasn't true?"

"Excellent! Mac is checking facts." She held up her finger and waited until she had everyone's full attention. "I gave you some *mis*information," she said, emphasizing *mis-*. "Father Louis Hennepin was the first *European* to see and describe Niagara Falls. But he wasn't the first person to see Niagara Falls. That would be the Native Americans who lived in our area. When facts are missing, it blurs the truth."

Students murmured.

"Also..." Mrs. Schieber paused again. "Part of the information I gave you about Hennepin was completely untrue."

The room buzzed.

"False information given on purpose is called *dis*information. It's meant to trick or mislead and that's serious."

Mrs. Schieber turned to Mac. "Would you like to research Father Hennepin? Figure out what information I gave was false?"

Mac raised both hands in the air. "I'm on it!"

The class roared, including Mrs. Schieber. She clicked the button and a website link and list of explorers appeared. "Fact detectives, copy this link. I'd like you to begin your research by visiting this website. Now, let's choose explorers and team up!"

Julian sat forward. Samuel de Champlain was on the list! Julian lived on Champlain Avenue. "Can I research Champlain?" he asked.

"You *may* research Champlain." Mrs. Schieber winked.

"Wait! I wanted Champlain."

Julian turned when he heard Maddie's voice. She swiped at her bangs. "My aunt lives in Quebec. We visited Lake Champlain last summer." She crossed her arms. "I want to research Champlain."

"Wonderful," declared Mrs. Schieber. "You may partner with Julian." She made a note and then looked across the room. "Are there any other requests?"

Chapter Nine

Clues

After school, Maya and Lacey hurried down the hall. They had only a few minutes before their bus would leave. The girls found Ms. Choi sitting at her desk. A heavy white book lay open in front of her.

"Maya!" she exclaimed. "I'm glad you stopped in. I am preparing for our next Make-and-Take project. What do you think about creating kindness rocks to leave along the sidewalks in our neighborhoods?"

Maya sprang onto her toes. "Kindness rocks!" She noticed the puzzled look on Lacey's face. "You decorate a rock and write a message that will brighten someone's day. That's why they're called kindness rocks." She looked to Ms. Choi, who nodded. "Then you leave the rock in a place where it's sure to be found." Maya clapped her hands. "I love that idea!"

"I had a hunch you would." Ms. Choi smiled. "I'm working on a set of directions and a list of supplies. "We need colorful paints that won't wash away when it rains. And rocks, of course." She turned to Lacey. "We can always use another helper if you'd like to join us."

Clues

A kindness rocks project sounded friendly and fun, but Lacey's mind was on mystery. "Actually, supplies are the reason we stopped by," she told Ms. Choi.

"That's right!" Maya's thoughts shifted away from kindness rocks. "Did you find the missing glitter pens?" she asked.

Ms. Choi shook her head. "I'm afraid I did not."

Maya's smile drooped, but almost as quickly lifted back into place. "Maybe we can help." Maya knew Lacey liked to begin at the beginning. "We take care of the Little Free Library in Cayuga Island Park," she began.

Lacey zeroed in. "There's a sharing notebook inside. It's for borrowers to leave notes about the books. One of the messages was written in glitter pen."

Ms. Choi waited for the girls to go on.

"We wondered." Maya shrugged. "Could the person who wrote the message have taken the missing glitter pens?"

Ms. Choi folded her hands. "Glitter pens are popular. They're easily found in craft stores and even drugstores. I don't think we can assume that whoever wrote in the sharing notebook took the club glitter pens." She looked from girl to girl. She smiled, but it was a small smile, not like the one she had on her face when she was talking about kindness rocks.

Maya realized Ms. Choi was right. She herself had an assortment of glitter pens in the craft drawer in her bedroom. Maya's shoulders slumped. "We jumped to conclusions."

"We just want to help," Lacey reasoned. She was ready to work on the case. "We could investigate who wrote the message. We have a few clues."

"Clues?" Ms. Choi's head tilted.

Lacey pulled the Little Free Library sharing notebook from her backpack. She opened to the page with the glitter pen message and offered it to Ms. Choi. "It's hard to read because the pages stuck together."

Maya leaned over the desk. "That could be a clue. Maybe the person hasn't used glitter pens much. Maybe they didn't know to wait for the ink to dry before closing the book."

"Some of the words are misspelled. That's a clue," said Lacey.

"The person drew a cat." Maya pointed to the picture. "It's such a cute cat!"

Ms. Choi studied the page in the notebook.

"The person really liked a book about pets," Lacey noted. "That's another clue."

Suddenly, Maya realized the halls were quiet. That was a clue! She pulled on Lacey's arm. "We have to catch our bus!"

Ms. Choi handed the sharing notebook to the girls. "Let me think about this before our next club meeting."

Maya's face lit up. "Kindness rocks! I can't wait. Would you like me to collect some rocks?"

"That's very *kind* of you." Ms. Choi's smile grew wide again.

"I'm going to put a kindness rock beside the Little Free Library!" Maya announced as the girls hurried out the door.

By the time they got to the bus, Maya was already thinking about what to write on her rock.

Chapter Ten

Plans

Mac's lunchbox clattered as he raced to catch up with Yoko. "Maya and I are going to the public library to work on our explorer project. Do you want to come?"

"I'd much rather practice gestures." Yoko shoved her hands in her pockets. Her shoulders rose to meet her ears. "But sure. I don't know much about explorers. And we got stuck with two! Lewis *and* Clark. At least I lucked out teaming with Lacey."

"I lucked out, too." Mac was thinking of Maya. "Julian, not so much." Mac was thinking of Maddie. At least he and Julian didn't have fractions homework tonight. They both lucked out there.

Yoko and Mac boarded the bus and found their friend hunched over his tablet. He was reading about Champlain, of course. Maya and Lacey rushed up the bus steps just before Mrs. O'Doodle cranked the door closed.

Once in their seats, the friends made plans to meet at the library.

"I guess I should invite Maddie," Julian mumbled. He busied himself with putting away his tablet.

Lacey harrumphed. "I wonder if Miss Information has some *mis*information to share about Champlain." Lacey emphasized *mis-* just as Mrs. Schieber had.

Yoko noticed bright spots like cinnamon balls colored Julian's cheeks. She scowled. "Grrr! I'm practicing my mad-at-Maddie face."

Julian knew his friends were thinking about his cookies and the cafeteria. "It'll be fine," he

Plans

said. He waved his hand as if having to team with Maddie was no big deal. But his forehead wrinkled as if it were.

Maya's eyes clouded with concern.

"Maddie *bugs* me." Mac slapped his neck, pretending to be swatting at a flying insect.

Lacey pulled out her magnifying glass and held it up as if inspecting Mac's neck.

"You both should try out for the school play!" exclaimed Yoko.

That brought a burst of giggles. Even Julian was smiling—all the way to his eyes.

Mac was glad. He liked it better when his friends were laughing than when they were frowning—even if they had good reason.

"Remember when Mrs. Schieber told us to be wise research explorers as we research our explorers?" Julian patted the pocket in his backpack that held his tablet. "When we get to the library, I want to show you something."

The door to the bus whined and slapped to a close. "Shoulders back, sit bones down! Buckle up, space cadets. This missile is about to blast off!" Mrs. O'Doodle began counting down from ten.

With two short beeps of the horn, and a wave to the crossing guard, Mrs. O'Doodle eased the bus away from the curb.

Chapter Eleven

Mis- Dis- Information

The kids gathered at their favorite study table in the far corner of the public library. Chairs bumped together in front of screens. Heads hovered over maps.

The kids read. They scratched notes.

And they laughed.

"That Mrs. Schieber!" exclaimed Mac. Then he remembered he was in the library. He lowered his voice. "Hennepin didn't invent the clothespin!"

"What?" Maddie huffed in disbelief. But Julian smiled.

"We're pretty sure Mrs. Schieber made that up," Maya confirmed. "We couldn't find anything about a hen's pin in the books about Hennepin."

"So we looked up the clothespin." Mac fanned the pages of a hefty book. "No sign of clothespins until the 1800s." His whisper grew louder. "Hennepin lived in the 1600s!"

"Mrs. Schieber wants us to research explorers. But more than that, she wants us to research facts." Lacey wiggled her pen between her fingers. "Be a fact detective," she murmured, repeating the words she had said in class.

Yoko pointed to Mac's book. "Mrs. Schieber wanted to see if you could figure out which 'facts' she shared were false." Yoko gestured with air quotes.

"*Dis*information," said Julian.

Maya rose and stood behind her chair. She placed her hand on the back and pointed her toes outward. "Mrs. Schieber told us about a book Hennepin wrote, *The New Discovery*. I figured it was about the hen's pin—or the clothespin."

"Me, too!" Yoko smacked her forehead. She knew that gesture was like saying, "Duh!"

"Hennepin did write that book," Mac said. "But it's about his explorations, not his laundry."

"Misinformation," said Julian.

Lacey agreed. "Part of what Mrs. Schieber said was true. But facts are missing, just like when she told us about Hennepin being the first to see Niagara Falls."

Maddie's fingers drummed the table. "Mrs. Schieber shouldn't share information that isn't true. What if we told other kids about the hen's pin?" Her eyes flashed. "If we said we heard it from a teacher, they would believe it, too." Maddie's voice rose. "If they told someone, and that person told someone else, pretty soon a bunch of people would think the clothespin was invented by Hennepin." She shook her head and her bangs swung across her forehead. "That's just not right."

The table grew silent.

The Cayuga Island Kids looked at each other and then their eyes rested on Julian.

They were all thinking about chocolate chip cookies.

Chapter Twelve

Fact Detectives

The Cayuga Island Kids looked from Julian to Maddie.

Maddie's eyes darted around the table. Her cheeks pinked. "Am I wrong about sharing false information?" she sputtered. Her chin jutted an inch higher.

"No, Maddie. You're right." Julian slid his tablet to the center of the table so everyone could see the screen. "On the bus I checked the website Mrs. Schieber gave us. I read about Champlain. Something didn't seem right, so I checked another source." He shrugged his shoulders and the corners of his mouth lifted. "And then I checked another one." Julian tapped and scrolled to a section he had highlighted. "This information about Champlain isn't true."

"So the website Mrs. Schieber told us to use has false facts, too?" Maddie leaned over and read the highlighted section aloud.

> CHAMPLAIN LEARNED TO NAVIGATE FROM HIS FATHER, A SEA CAPTAIN. A NAVIGATION SYSTEM CALLED RADAR HAD BEEN INVENTED JUST BEFORE HE SAILED TO THE SPANISH COLONIES IN NORTH AMERICA BETWEEN 1599 AND 1601.

Lacey burst out laughing. "I'm not sure exactly when radar was invented, but it wasn't in the 1600s!"

"It was invented in the 1900s." Julian scrolled up the page. "Most of the information about Champlain on this website is true. But some of it is false."

"Tricky," mused Mac. No wonder Mrs.

Schieber was one of his favorite teachers.

"It's sort of funny because obviously it's not true," said Maya. "But false information that isn't obvious isn't so funny. It can hurt." She faced Maddie and spoke softly. "Remember when you said the specks in Julian's cookies were flour bugs?"

Maddie stiffened. "I read about flour bugs on the internet. They're real. I saw pictures!"

"We saw them, too." Maya grimaced.

"You told me to look them up," Julian reminded Maddie. "We did."

"It's true that flour bugs can look like specks in cookies," said Yoko. "But not all specks in cookies are flour bugs."

"So, then, they could have been bugs!" Maddie voice was pinched.

"We learned some other facts from Julian's dad," said Maya.

"He's kind of an expert on flour," explained Mac.

"We investigated Julian's flour." Lacey patted the pocket holding her magnifying glass. "No bugs."

Maddie groaned. "I told Minh!" She cradled her chin in her hand. Her voice grew small. "I didn't mean to spread false information." Her eyes reddened. "I really didn't mean to hurt your feelings, Julian."

Maya put a hand on Maddie's arm. "You read something and then you saw something, and you jumped to conclusions." Suddenly, the sharing notebook came to mind.

"We all jumped to conclusions," admitted Yoko, remembering the uneaten cookies on the lunchroom table.

Maddie lowered her head onto her arms. "I'm really, really sorry!"

Mac shrugged his shoulders and held out his hands. "Everybody makes mistakes."

"My dad says mistakes are how we learn," said Julian. "But usually he's talking about cookie recipes."

Fact Detectives

Maddie raised her head and found Julian's grin. She laughed along with the others.

"We're learning to be fact detectives," Lacey said.

"I'll set the facts straight with Minh," Maddie promised.

Lacey held up her hand to Maddie.

High-fives circled the table. But the friends slapped softly. They were in the library, after all.

CHAPTER THIRTEEN

Suspect

On their way out of the library, the kids passed the community room.

Maya heard mewing and stopped to peek inside. She pulled on Lacey's arm. "Miss Lynne's here with her scout troop!"

Their neighbor was at the check-in table. She waved them in and Maya hurried around the table to give her a hug.

Miss Lynne spoke in a low voice. "My troop is very excited. Today we have a guest from the animal shelter."

The young scouts crowded on the floor in front of a short round table. A woman in a jacket

Suspect

with an emblem on her shoulder stood before them.

Inside a wire cage on the table was a rumpled blue blanket. It moved, and out from under it wiggled two kittens. One was cream-colored, like vanilla ice cream. The other was black, with a spike of fur between its ears.

The woman patted the top of the cage. She leaned down, looking from girl to girl. "Are you ready to learn how to properly handle a kitten?"

The scouts clapped and cheered, but quickly quieted when the woman held a finger to her lips. "We don't want to frighten the kittens." She spoke in a low voice. "Tip number one. Talk softly and move slowly when approaching a cat that does not know you."

A hand shot up in the air. "I love kitties! I wish I could have one, but my brother is allergic."

Even from the back, Maya could see the colorful beads on the girl's tumble of braids. *Kittens would love how those dance when she moves*, Maya thought. She knew her cat Sparky would!

The woman opened the cage door slowly and the black kitten scampered toward her. His tail shot up and he rubbed his face against her hand. "This is Milo," she said.

"He likes you!" declared a girl sitting on her knees.

Meanwhile, the other kitten's body hung low as she slinked forward. Her tail swished.

"She's nervous," Maya whispered to Lacey.

Right then, the woman said, "This is Ophelia. She's uneasy."

"We should get going," Lacey said.

"It was nice to see you both," Miss Lynne whispered.

Just then a scout pushed the door open and rushed inside. "I'm late!" she announced. A gust of wind swept into the room. It blew across the check-in table, and a stack of papers scattered.

The girl wrung her hands. "I'm sorry!" She looked from Miss Lynne to the woman holding the kitten.

Miss Lynne patted the girl's shoulder. "Go on and sit down. I'll have these picked up in a jiffy."

Lacey and Maya hurried to help Miss Lynne. The girl with the colorful braids jumped up to return a paper that had landed near her foot.

Lacey crawled under the table to reach another paper.

She stared at the sparkly drawing.

Lacey showed the note to Maya before placing it on the pile.

"That one's mine!" the girl announced proudly.

She took a few steps toward the group and then stopped. She turned and looked closely at Maya. "Aren't you Ms. Choi's helper in Make-and-Take Club?"

Maya read the girl's nametag. Taishi. She recalled the name from Ms. Choi's check-in list. Suddenly, Maya recognized her. Ms. Choi had remarked on how well her purple beaded headband matched the apron she had chosen from the hooks beside the supply closet. "Did you pick that apron on purpose?" Ms. Choi had kidded.

"Of course!" the girl had answered. "It's purple!" Maya remembered thinking her laugh sounded like a bubbly waterfall.

"I love Make-and-Take Club!" Taishi whispered. "Almost as much as I love kitties!" Her giggle followed her as she skipped back to join the group.

Chapter Fourteen
Meet at the Scene

The next afternoon, Lacey hurried down the aisle of the bus toward her friends. She waved her notebook above her head. "We have more clues to the mystery!"

"We still haven't heard the first clues," Mac reminded her.

"Right." Lacey drew her notebook in close. "You will find out everything when we meet at the scene."

"The scene?" Julian was curious. "Like in a crime?"

"The scene?" Yoko echoed. "Like in a play?"

"The Little Free Library," Lacey replied. "The scene where we found the clues."

Meet at the Scene

"Clues to the mystery—that we'll tell you all about." Maya assured Mac. Then she answered Julian. "Clues to a crime. Well, sort of a crime. Maybe."

Then Maya zipped her lips. If she kept on talking, she'd tell them everything, including some details that probably weren't important.

Yesterday, after they left the scout meeting, she and Lacey had agreed on a plan. They would meet their friends at the Little Free Library in the park where they could look at the sharing notebook, talk through the clues, and brainstorm ideas.

"Adventure awaits!" Mac unloaded his backpack from his shoulder. That's when he remembered his fractions homework buried inside.

Yesterday, Ms. Spritski had given them one night off from math homework to work on their explorer projects—but one night only. "Your math brains will get rusty if you don't practice," she declared.

Mac sank into his seat. Adventure might have to wait.

Julian figured only fractions could cause Mac to slump like that. "Let's work on our homework together," he suggested to his friend. "You can sample the new batch of cookies Dad and I made last night while we tackle the fractions."

Mac brightened. "Your cookies make fractions a whole lot easier to take."

Meet at the Scene

Julian invited the others to come, too.

But Lacey had to clean her room and brush Pesky before she could go to the park. Or maybe, she would brush Pesky and then clean her room.

Maya had promised to collect rocks for Ms. Choi's Make-and-Take Club project.

And Yoko wanted to practice a few more of the gestures displayed on the poster she had hung in her room before she headed to the park. She planned to memorize them all. She might even try out a few when they met at the scene.

"Hit the mute button on your amplifiers!" Mrs. O'Doodle commanded from the front of the bus. "We are about to rock and roll—silent movie style!"

The friends quickly agreed on a time to gather at the Little Free Library and took their seats.

Gestures

Chapter Fifteen

Feeling Good

Mac was on his way to Julian's house. The fur tail on his coonskin cap swished in a friendly way. It wasn't really fur, and Mac liked that. His powder horn swung from his shoulder. It was much lighter than his backpack had been, and Mac liked that, too.

When he thought about his backpack, Mac realized he had forgotten to take his fraction worksheet out of it before he set off for Julian's house.

Stink bug! He was almost halfway there!

Dark clouds seem to hang above Mac's head anytime fractions were involved.

Not so for Ms. Spritski. Math made his teacher feel good, like dancing made Maya feel, or collecting clues made Lacey feel.

Every day Ms. Spritski reminded her students, "Math is all around us!" And she wasn't talking about the math posters hanging on every wall in their classroom. She reminded them when she collected lunch money each morning to deliver to the cafeteria. And when they lined up in "two equal lines" to go to lunch. When the class groaned about math homework, she'd say, "Get to know math, and math will be your friend."

Mac was trying to be friends with math. But right now, math equaled fractions. And they were not friendly. Right now, the math all around him was **M**ental **A**gony **T**orturing **H**umans.

Mac sighed and hurried back home. The sooner he got to Julian's house, the sooner he'd get one of Julian's chocolate chip cookies. At least he hoped he was going to get a whole cookie from the new batch, and not just a fraction of one.

After the homework and cookies were finished, Julian and Mac would meet up with their friends—their real friends—at the Little Free Library in the park.

He was wondering about the clues Lacey and Maya had to share as he walked back into his house.

In the kitchen, Mac's sister Sookie was searching deep in a bottom cupboard. She lifted her head and pointed at the counter. "You forgot to clean out your lunchbox."

Stink bug x 2! Mac trudged to the sink.

"It's your turn to set the table tonight." Sookie's head was inside the cupboard again, but Mac heard her just fine. "Dad's out of town, but Mom invited Miss Lynne for dinner."

"Mom says homework first," Mac reminded his sister. He fished inside his backpack. "What are we having for dinner, anyway?"

Sookie's head popped up. "Roasted vegetables and rice," she answered. "If I can find the roasting pan, that is."

Mac's nose wrinkled. "Maybe you should give up looking for the pan and do *your* homework," Mac suggested. "We could always order a pizza from Buzzy's."

"Hmmm." Sookie rocked back on her heels. "We could order the large pie. Do you think eight slices would be enough?"

"There will be four of us, so that's two pieces each." Mac pictured Buzzy's steaming cheesy pizza. Then Ms. Spritski's plastic pizza came to mind. They would each get ¼ of the pizza.

Sookie stood and brushed off her knees. "I'll text Mom and see what she says. I can make a salad with the veggies."

Mac didn't answer. He was on his way out the door. He wanted to get to Julian's house while his brain was still warmed up. He had just figured out a fraction! Mac smiled and tugged on his cap. He was feeling good.

Chapter Sixteen

Clue Review

The Cayuga Island Kids gathered around the Little Free Library.

While Pesky nosed the grass, Lacey opened the sharing notebook to the page with the messy message.

They agreed with Maya. The kitty drawing was cute.

"Those Pet Care Adventure books were as good as buttered toast," Yoko recalled. "The kitten in the story looked so soft and fluffy." She gave herself a hug. "I just wanted to reach inside the book and snuggle it."

"Why is the message so blurry?" asked Mac. "Is that the mystery?"

Clue Review

"The messy message is not the mystery." Lacey opened her notebook. "But it could be a clue."

Maya explained the best way to use glitter pens. "Always remember to let the ink dry," she warned.

Lacey clicked her pen and then clicked it again. "The main thing is that the mystery has to do with missing glitter pens."

"We're calling it the Make-and-Take Club Mystery because it all started in Ms. Choi's after school craft club." Maya figured that was important.

"What started in craft club?" Julian was looking for facts.

Lacey looked at Maya. After all, she was the witness. She had been there. "Will you explain what happened? The important details?" she asked.

So Maya did.

Afterwards, Lacey read from her notebook.

The Make-and-Take Club Mystery

** What happened to the missing glitter pens??? **

CLUES

Two glitter pens missing at the end of the Make-and-Take Club meeting

Messy message in sharing notebook written with glitter pen (Maybe person hasn't used glitter pens much? Doesn't know to wait for ink to dry?)

Misspelled words in messy message: realy, luv, storry, kittys

The person who wrote the messy message drew a cat. The drawing could help us figure out who wrote the message.

The person really liked a book about pets.

Maya sighed. "I really want us to find those two missing glitter pens for Ms. Choi. Without them, she will have to buy another whole set to be able to have two glitter pens for each kid."

Yoko held her hands wide. "You've collected a slew of clues!"

"But will they lead to the missing glitter pens?" Julian wondered.

Lacey smiled. "There's more." She flipped the page in her notebook and turned to Maya again. "Tell them what happened at the scout meeting. The important parts."

Meanwhile, Lacey checked her notes.

SUSPECT

The person who drew the cat in the sharing notebook (Taishi) was at the scout meeting.

We know Taishi drew the cat in the sharing notebook because she drew the same picture of a cat on a thank you note for the scout meeting guest (who brought two kittens).

Clue Review

CLUES

Taishi is in Ms. Choi's Make-and-Take Club.
kittys, luv-misspelled in the thank you note just like in the sharing notebook.

"Now we're onto something!" Mac didn't know much about glitter pens, but he was always ready to solve a mystery with his friends. "You have a kitty drawing match!"

"And a misspelled words match." Yoko's eyebrows bounced above her sunglasses.

"Another important fact..." Julian tapped Lacey's notebook. "The clues lead to a suspect who was at the scene of the crime."

"We are Fact Detectives!" Lacey exclaimed.

Pesky wagged his tail at the sparkle in Lacey's voice. The friends cheered. Everyone except Maya.

She was quiet. And she wasn't pointing her toes or practicing a new dance step.

That was a clue.

CHAPTER SEVENTEEN

Important?

Something was bothering Maya.

"The clues point to Taishi as the person who wrote the message in the sharing notebook. But that doesn't mean she took the glitter pens." Maya's eyes met Lacey's. "Remember what Ms. Choi said. Glitter pens are common. Lots of people have them." She looked from friend to friend. "Are we jumping to conclusions?" she asked.

Before anyone could answer, Mr. Esposito chugged up the path in his golf cart-turned-gardening cart. Rakes of different sizes rattled in the back. His brakes groaned as he pulled to a stop and hopped out.

Pesky wiggled and wagged until Mr. Esposito bent to give him a pat. Then he sat and wiggled and wagged while Mr. Esposito fished a dog treat from one of the pockets in his gardener's apron.

"When I was raking here earlier I found something on the ground." Mr. Esposito patted the other apron pockets. "Too many pockets," he mumbled. Finally, he pulled out a wide purple headband decorated with sparkly beads. "I'm afraid it's a bit muddy from the rain last night."

"Is that yours?" Julian asked Maya. It was a fact that purple was her favorite color.

Maya shook her head. "It's not mine. But I'm pretty sure I know who it belongs to." She paused. "Taishi was wearing a headband just like this at Make-and-Take Club."

"Would you like to return it to her?" Mr. Esposito asked.

Maya accepted the headband from Mr. Esposito. She held it by its edges, careful not to rub the smudges of dirt. She knew from her mom that you had to be patient. Let mud dry, and ballet shoes are much easier to clean. She figured it was the same for headbands.

Mac tugged on his cap. "Another clue!"

Lacey was already writing in her notebook.

"Clue?" repeated Mr. Esposito.

"We're working on another mystery." Yoko tapped the side of her head to gesture that they were thinking.

"Something's missing," said Julian. "Actually

two things." He liked to stick to the facts.

Mr. Esposito tipped his cap. "I'm confident you will solve the mystery. Is there anything I can do to help?"

Lacey pointed to the headband. "You already did. You found evidence."

Mr. Esposito dug around in his apron pockets for another treat for Pesky before he drove off.

Suddenly, Maya gasped. She rose onto her toes and then sank into her heels. "The aprons!" she exclaimed.

"Aprons?" Mac repeated.

"We wear aprons in Make-and Take Club!" Maya held her hands to her cheeks.

"You make snacks in Make-and-Take Club?"

"Craft aprons," Maya clarified. "The kids wear aprons so they don't get glue or paint or marker on their clothes. They put them on at the start of the meeting and hang them on the hooks at the end."

"Is that important?" asked Lacey.

"I don't know." Maya shoulders drooped.

Yoko patted Maya on the back. She knew that gesture between friends could help.

"When I saw Mr. Esposito searching through his apron pockets, I remembered. Ms. Choi looked in her pockets for the missing glitter pens. But we didn't check the kids' aprons."

"They have pockets, too?" asked Julian.

Maya nodded, her eyes wide.

Lacey paged through her notes. "We have clues. We have evidence. It all points to Taishi." She frowned and fingered her notebook. "But maybe," she said slowly, "we don't have all the facts."

Lacey slid the notebook in her pocket. "Let's see what we find out at Make-and-Take Club tomorrow."

Chapter Eighteen

Fraction of the Truth

Mac was eager for his turn at Supper Share. Each night at the dinner table, everyone shared something they had learned that day. Often, Mac had to dive deep into his brain for a clue about what to share. But not tonight. He would talk about the Make-and-Take Club Mystery.

Miss Lynne arrived with a large pot of spaghetti with red sauce just as Mac's mom was placing the pizza and salad on the table. "An Italian Feast!" she declared.

Sookie began Supper Share by explaining what she had learned about black holes. Sookie loved science as much as Julian did, and ever since school started, she had shared a fact from class at the dinner table.

Meanwhile, Mac eyed the pizza. He zeroed in on the piece he was hoping for. It was loaded with cheese bubbles. He picked and poked at his salad. He pushed the carrot slices beneath the biggest piece of lettuce and then smooshed the leaf flat. There was not a clue that carrots were hiding there. He ate the tiny tomatoes, though. They were sweet and juicy and that's why they were his favorite vegetable.

Mom shared next. She told a joke she had heard on the radio. While everyone laughed, she passed the pizza around the table.

Mac slid the piece of pizza he had eyed onto his plate. He was eager for his turn at Supper Share. But he really wanted to eat his pizza while it was still warm and gooey. "You can go before me, Miss Lynne," he offered.

"No, no!" Miss Lynne waved her hand. "I want to wait until everyone has had a chance to taste my sauce. I promised your mom I'd reveal my secret ingredient." She leaned over the pasta bowl and inhaled. "It's something that's often missing from spaghetti sauce."

"Mysterious," said Mac. "Like the Make-and-Take Club Mystery." He took a bite of pizza. Buzzy's was the best!

"Tell us," Sookie prompted.

Mac described the messy message in the Little Free Library sharing notebook. He recounted the clues Lacey and Maya had collected. When Mac told them about Taishi's thank you note at the scout meeting, Miss Lynne nodded. She had been there, of course. Finally, Mac mentioned the headband Mr. Esposito found in the park. "It's evidence!" he said.

"That's impressive detective work," Miss Lynne commented. "And I'm glad to know you're calling Taishi a *suspect*."

Mac was confused. *Why was Miss Lynne glad Taishi was a suspect?*

Miss Lynne seemed to read Mac's mind. "You have information—or clues. It's likely that Taishi wrote the note in the sharing notebook." She paused.

"But you don't know for sure," Sookie piped up.

"I was getting to that." Mac made a scrunchy face at Sookie.

His mom pinned him with her eyes.

"More importantly," Miss Lynne continued, "you're missing facts that *prove* Taishi took Ms. Choi's glitter pens."

"That's what Maya said," Mac admitted. "Tomorrow at the Make-and-Take Club meeting, Maya and Lacey are going to check something."

"Sounds mysterious," Sookie said. "Tell us."

"You'll have to wait until Supper Share tomorrow night to find out," Mac answered, and when his mother wasn't looking he crossed his eyes at his sister.

Miss Lynne scooped pasta onto everyone's plate. "Gathering all the facts—instead of just a fraction of the truth—is smart. And it's the right thing to do."

Mac thought back to Maddie's fraction of the truth about flour bugs and Mrs. Schieber's fraction of the truth about Champlain being the first to see Niagara Falls. Both had blurred the truth.

He twirled the pasta onto his fork and took a bite. The sauce was sweet and fresh. Instantly, he forgot about fractions, and about not talking with his mouth full. "This is really, really good," he murmured.

"Yum!" Sookie agreed.

"Delish!" Mac's mom leaned across the table toward their neighbor. "So what's the secret ingredient?"

Miss Lynne held her hand to her mouth as if she were sharing a secret. "Shredded carrots," she said.

Chapter Nineteen

Mystery Solved

After school, Lacey helped Maya carry the rocks to Ms. Choi's room. Maya had chosen only those she thought would be perfect to decorate. But she had collected plenty.

"Hello, my friends!" Ms. Choi greeted the girls. When Maya showed her all the shapes and sizes of the rocks, she smiled. "I know I can always count on you."

Ms. Choi reached for her supply list. "Lacey, would you please get the paints and brushes from the storage closet?"

Lacey opened the tall double doors. On the

The Cayuga Island Kids

shelf in front of her was the glitter pen tray with two pens missing.

"We have more clues," she told Ms. Choi. "About the missing glitter pens."

Ms. Choi looked up from the rocks she and Maya were arranging on the table.

"We have evidence," Lacey added. "It points to a suspect."

Maya eyed the row of aprons. "But we want to check something first."

Just then three of the young crafters entered the room. Two were holding hands and the third led the way in his wheelchair. One of the kids was Taishi.

When she spotted Maya and Lacey, she skipped across the room. "Hi! Remember me?"

Maya unzipped her backpack and pulled out the purple beaded headband. It was clean, with just one tiny mark on the underside. "Is this yours?" she asked.

Mystery Solved

Taishi's bubbly laugh filled the room as she took the headband from Maya. "I thought it was lost forever!" She held it to her chest. "Where did you find it?" she asked.

"In the park by the Little Free Library," Lacey said.

"I love the Little Free Library!" Taishi placed the beaded headband beside the purple-striped one already on her head. "These match the purple craft apron," she said, eying the hooks holding the aprons. "That one's my favorite."

Lacey knew Maya was eager to check the aprons. But she had to know. "Did you write a message in the Little Free Library sharing notebook?" she blurted.

"Yes!" Taishi said. "I borrowed the pet care adventure books. I finished the one about chickens, and now I'm reading one about a hamster. But the book about the kitty is my favorite." She paused. "I love kitties. But we can't have one because my brother is allergic."

"I remember you us told that," said Maya. "I have a cat. Maybe someday you could come over. Her name is Sparky, and she likes purple as much as we do!" Maya hesitated and looked at Lacey. Taishi didn't act guilty when they mentioned the Little Free Library sharing notebook. Should they ask her about the glitter pen she used to write the message?

Mystery Solved

Meanwhile, the rest of the Make-and-Take Club kids were gathering in the room. Ms. Choi signaled to Maya. "Could you please help with the aprons? Get our crafters settled?" she asked.

Taishi raced to grab the purple apron. Maya and Lacey followed. But it was too late to check the pockets of the aprons. The kids jumbled together, pulling aprons from the hooks.

A girl tugged on Maya's arm. "Will you tie this for me?" she asked.

Lacey knelt to help another girl having trouble with a tight snap.

A boy stamped his foot. "This apron has a knot!"

Finally, all the kids were seated with their aprons tied, buttoned, or snapped. Ms. Choi held up her hand. It was the signal for "Quiet."

She began to explain about kindness rocks when suddenly a boy at the last table shouted, "Ms. Choi! Look what I found in my apron pocket!"

He held up two glitter pens.

Chapter Twenty

Kindness Rocks

Early Saturday morning Julian waited for his friends beside the Little Free Library. It was cool, but the sun was shining through the brightly colored leaves.

Julian had been so busy with cookie recipes, fraction worksheets, and the explorer project that he hadn't had time to find answers to his questions about leaves changing color in the fall.

He was reading his tablet when Mac arrived. "Listen to this!" he said.

"In the fall, chlorophyll in leaves breaks down. As this happens, other colors beside green come through. Leaves finally show their reds, yellows, and oranges— the colors that were always there in the first place."

"So the colors hide until it's time to make like a tree and leave." Mac grinned when his friend rolled his eyes.

Julian looked across the park to the creek. "Science is all around us," he said.

"You sound like Ms. Spritski talking about math," said Mac. He reached inside his powder horn and pulled out a pack of puffy fish stickers. "Do you want half?" he asked and then he realized. That was math!

Soon, Lacey and Yoko arrived.

"I've memorized all the gestures on my wall chart." Yoko pumped her fist. "I'm going to practice them all the way up until the day of the school play tryouts."

"Practice on us," Julian suggested. "After all, I practice cookie recipes on you." He reached inside his backpack and offered a cookie to each of his friends.

Yoko made an "okay" gesture because her mouth was full of cookie.

So was Mac's. But he talked anyway. "These are the best ones so far!"

"Dad found a recipe from a woman who won a cookie contest. Her secret is rolling the cookies instead of spooning them onto the cookie sheet." He held his cookie up. "They brown on the outside and stay soft in the middle."

Yoko rubbed her stomach. She sighed deeply and closed her eyes.

"You like your cookie. Right?" A smile tugged at the corner of Julian's mouth.

"The only thing missing is the bugs," joked Mac.

He was brushing away crumbs when Maya skipped up the path. "Sorry I'm late!" She paused to catch her breath. "Taishi stopped by to meet Sparky. I never heard that cat purr so much! I told Taishi she can be Sparky's aunt. Then I showed her my craft drawer. I lost track of time."

Julian handed Maya a cookie. She held it to her nose to smell its goodness before she bit into it.

"I have books to donate!" Mrs. Schieber announced as she wheeled up on her bike. "Then I have to run. Saturday is errands day!"

Julian reached into his bag. He always packed an extra cookie. He offered it to Mrs. Schieber, and after one bite she declared it, "stupendous!" She asked Julian if he would share the recipe.

She placed her books in the Little Free Library and then plucked a biography from the shelf. Lacey recognized it as one Gram had donated.

"I'm looking forward to Monday when I find out what facts my research explorers have discovered," said Mrs. Schieber.

"Me, too!" said Julian. He and Maddie had agreed to finish up their report tomorrow.

Mrs. Schieber was about to hop on her bike when her foot bumped against something nestled in the leaves. She reached down and picked it up. "Well, look at that!" she marveled. "A pretty rock that says, "Do your best. Forget the rest."

Kindness Rocks

"That's a kindness rock," said Maya. "You can keep it."

"Kindness *rocks*." Mrs. Schieber waited for the kids to get her play on words before heading down the path.

Maya finished her cookie and smacked her lips. "This is the best chocolate chip cookie ever," she said.

"No need for further investigation?" asked Julian.

"Well," said Mac, "we wouldn't mind if you wanted to keep working on recipes."

"I'm just happy we don't need to keep working on The Make-and-Take Club Mystery," said Maya. "Taishi didn't take Ms. Choi's glitter pens. And I'm glad."

Lacey sighed. "The clues and evidence pointed to Taishi. But I didn't have all the facts."

"I'm working on making better cookies. You're working on being a better fact detective," said Julian, nudging Lacey's shoulder.

"I'm working on being better friends with math," said Mac.

Yoko lifted her hand to her forehead and wiped away imaginary sweat. "We're all working on something," she said.

Maya tucked her arm through Lacey's. "Do your best. Forget the rest."

Lacey liked that. "I'll do my best not to jump to conclusions," she vowed.

Kindness Rocks

"Speaking of jumping…" Mac pointed to the rocks by the creek. "Adventures await!"

The Cayuga Island Kids played in the park for the rest of the day. They hopped across the rocks by the creek. Julian gathered leaves for an experiment. Maya gathered some, too, for a placemat craft. Pesky just chased the leaves.

Yoko practiced acting happy, sad, confused, and sleepy. She used gestures and her friends guessed her feelings. Lacey declared she was giving excellent clues.

As the sun dipped behind the trees, the Cayuga Island Kids set off for home. On the way, they passed the Little Free Library. Maya remembered the pen strap tucked in her pocket. She had made it from purple ribbon. Ms. Choi had shown her the perfect way to secure the pen to the sharing notebook.

When Maya unlatched the library door, she discovered something resting on the shelf.

Turn the page to see a photo of the real Pesky and to find the Story Behind the Story of the

Cayuga Island Kids

series!

The Story Behind the Story

Although the Cayuga Island Kids series is fictional, many aspects of the stories come from real life.

The **setting**, or where the Cayuga Island Kids series takes place, is real. The island is located a few miles upstream from the mighty Niagara Falls. I grew up there, and my observations, along with memories, helped me form ideas for the stories in this series.

The **characters** in the Cayuga Island Kids series are **fictional**. They are not real children

The Story Behind the Story

or adults. However, my characters are based on people I know or have observed. My brother inspired Mac.

The author's brother Anthony, age 7

Pesky is based on a dog named Genna.

Genna, 2020

My cousin is a college professor and an excellent cook. She inspired Miss Lynne. Mrs. Schieber is based on a friend. She is not a librarian, but she loves to read, research, and bake. There's also a bit of me in every character. Check out the photo from when I was about the age of the Cayuga Island Kids. Does this remind you of anyone?

The author, age 8

The events in this story came from my imagination. The ideas, however, came from my interests, observations, and experiences:

- I am a big fan and supporter of **Little Free Libraries**. These community libraries can be found in neighborhoods everywhere. Readers may take and also give books. I am always on the lookout for Little Free Libraries when I travel, and I have discovered many creative free libraries. I even found one in a tiny restaurant in Torino, Italy!

Little library in a restaurant in Torino, Italy, 2018

A collection of photos of LFLs can be found on my website in the FAQ section. You can build a Little Free Library for your front yard or anywhere people will find it. Be creative! For more information, visit littlefreelibrary.org .

- During the Covid-19 pandemic, **kindness rocks** became a way for people to lift the spirits of others in their neighborhood or community. While I was writing this story in the midst of the pandemic, I found a kindness rock under a tree in my front yard.

Later, a kindness rock was placed in one of the Little Free Libraries for which I provide books. What's funny is that it was found *after* I had written the scene where the kindness rock is discovered in the LFL in Cayuga Island Park!

Kindness rock found in a Little Free Library

- During the time I was writing this book, I became curious about **misinformation** and **disinformation**. When I am interested in something, I try to learn as much as I can about it. So I attended webinars, read books, sifted through articles, and thought about how the Cayuga Island Kids could face and deal with information that blurs the truth, or gives only some of the facts. Just because something appears in print or on the internet doesn't mean it's factual. When you hear or read something, determine if it's true before you repeat it. Being a fact detective is important.

- The chocolate chip cookie recipe that follows is a tasty fact. It is the creation of my friend, Mary Beth. When I was writing this story, I needed a recipe for Julian to try that would top all the others. I love to cook, but I am not a baker like Julian. I am more a taster like Julian's friends, and Mary Beth's cookies are the BEST. I requested her secret recipe as I was writing the ending of this story, and she gave me permission to share it with you.

Do you want to learn more about misinformation, disinformation, Little Free Libraries, flour bugs, or cookie variables? Do you want to know how to craft a kindness rock? Are you curious about gestures and facial expressions? I learned about all of these things and more as I wrote this book. Research is fun! Investigate topics that spark your interest in your school or public library and on safe online sites, just as the Cayuga Island Kids do. Be a fact detective. Always check more than one source. Make sure information is accurate.

Adventures await! Be curious, like the Cayuga Island Kids. And above all, be kind and be a good friend.

Find Activities and an Educator's Guide for this book and others in the Cayuga Island Kids series at **www.judybradbury.com** *and on* **www.CityofLightPublishing.com**.

Mary Beth's Magnificent Chocolate Chip Cookies

ingredients

- 4 sticks salted butter (room temperature, not melted)
- 1 ½ cups white sugar
- 1 ½ cups light brown sugar
- 4 eggs lightly beaten
- 4 teaspoons vanilla extract (do not use imitation vanilla)
- 5 ½ cups flour (loosely scooped, not packed)
- 2 teaspoons baking soda
- 1 teaspoon salt
- 36 ounces semisweet chocolate chips

other

- Use convection oven, if available
- Bake on parchment paper
- Makes about 36 good-sized cookies

Happy Baking! Be sure to have an adult help you.

steps

1. Cream softened (room temperature) butter. It should cream easily.
2. Add white and light brown sugar and mix until smooth.
3. Mix in eggs and vanilla.
4. Add flour, baking soda, and salt; mix well. You may mix with (clean!) hands.
5. Gently add chocolate chips either with a spatula or with your hands.
6. Roll the cookie dough into balls. This helps keep the center soft. **This is the secret to making magnificent chocolate chip cookies!*
7. Place on parchment paper on cookie sheets. (Parchment paper is key!) The dough will not spread much when baking.
8. Bake in a convection oven, if available, at 375 degrees Fahrenheit for 10-11 minutes. Baking time will vary in a conventional oven. Cookies will continue to harden as they set. Don't overbake, especially if you like cookies with a soft center.

Cayuga Island Kids

Book One

The Mystery of the Barking Branches and the Sunken Ship

What happens when a group of friends sets off on a hunt for a certain kind of tree and uncover a buried cannonball instead? Who knew that the island they live on is also home to a whole lot of history? And, it turns out, a whole lot of mystery, too… Meet the Cayuga Island Kids! It's summer vacation, and that means there's plenty of time for a hunt, a mystery, and an exciting adventure. Are you ready? Open the book and join the fun. Find out what the Cayuga Island Kids are up to in this mystery story based on historical events on Cayuga Island near Niagara Falls!

Book Two

The Adventure of the Big Fish by the Small Creek

It all begins one mid-summer day. First, the Cayuga Island Kids rescue a mallard caught in the plastic rings from six-pack of cans. Litter. Moments later, a girl on a bike carelessly tosses a plastic bottle in the creek. The Cayuga Island Kids successfully retrieve it, but then they notice all the litter in the park. That's when they decide it's time for action. But moving from knowing something has to be done to getting it done takes determination, teamwork, and sometimes, looking in a new direction. How the Cayuga Island Kids go from fishing a plastic bottle out of the creek to bringing the community together to build a recycling bin big enough to hold plenty of plastic makes for a lively adventure. Best of all, readers will cheer on the Cayuga Island Kids as they come to realize that although we are each just one person, together we can make a BIG difference.

Meet the Author

Judy Bradbury is an author, an award-winning literacy advocate and educator, and host of the popular Children's Book Corner blog. She is also a Cayuga Island Kid. Judy grew up on the island, which is located just a few miles upstream from the mighty Niagara Falls. In the summers, she rode the bicycle her father built for her across the island in search of mysteries to solve. Judy loves visiting schools and libraries to share her books with students, and frequently offers writing workshops.

Meet the Illustrator

Although she has always loved to draw, Gabriella Vagnoli became an illustrator via a circuitous route that allowed her to explore many other interests including theater, music, teaching, and languages. Her work in these fields all had a common thread: communication. And this is what she loves best about illustrating children's books—the opportunity to visually communicate a story in a way that will indelibly imprint it on young minds, just as she still has with her the illustrated stories from her childhood in Italy.